THE WAR OF 3021 A.D- A SPACE ODYSSEY

ARYAN KUMAR

Made with ♥ on the Notion Press Platform
www.notionpress.com

Contents

Acknowledgements

Writing this book has been an incredible journey, and it would not have been possible without the support of many individuals. First and foremost, I want to thank my parents, whose unwavering belief in me has been a constant source of strength and inspiration. Their love and encouragement have guided me through every challenge.

I also extend my heartfelt gratitude to my friends, who provided invaluable motivation and ideas. Their feedback and enthusiasm kept me going, especially during the tough times.

Lastly, I want to acknowledge the incredible community of science fiction writers and enthusiasts. Your creativity and vision continue to shape and expand the genre, and I am honoured to contribute to this vibrant world.

Prologue

In 2578 A.D., humanity made a ground-breaking discovery: wormholes, tunnels through space and time, connecting distant points in the universe. This technological leap into hyperspace travel propelled humanity into a new era, transforming the face of civilization and the galaxy itself. Cities now run entirely on sustainable power sources, and Mars has been colonized to alleviatc Earth's population burden. Inter-species relations flourished until the Intergalactic War of 2819 A.D., a dark era ignited by power conflicts. The Domicans, one faction, sought to establish a galaxy-wide dictatorship, while the Earth Federation and its allies advocated for democracy and free will. Post-war, the culprits faced heavy sanctions, restoring peace for 202 years. But in 3021 A.D., sinister plans set by the Domicans began to unfold once again...

CHAPTER ONE

CHAPTER 1: THE AWAKENING

3021 AD, Earth Federation

A light blue speeder, almost merging with the morning sky, sped past Capitol High towards the main docks of D.E.L.H.I, the capital of New India on Mars. It had been over 800 years since humans first colonized Mars. Initially, they lived in underground cities, slowly terraforming Mars into a green planet. Life outside our Solar System was discovered in the distant and innumerable systems of our vast galaxy. This was all thanks to the invention of hyperspace travel and wormholes. To the rest of the universe, Mars and Earth together are known as the Earth Federation. There have been good relations and even trade between humans and other species. There has been no war since the Treaty of Alkasan on the homeworld of the Terramanes, a humanoid species almost a foot smaller than the average human but hundreds of years ahead of us. This treaty took place after the great intergalactic war in 2819 AD, thus ending the conflict. According to the treaty, sanctions were imposed on the planets found guilty of aggression that escalated the war to a galactic level.

Achal Mehta, owner of A-Z Securities Pvt. Ltd., stood at the main docks, his eyes scanning the horizon. His mind was a whirlwind of thoughts as he waited for news about the shipment. A tall, well-built man in his mid-forties, Achal's presence commanded respect. His brownish eyes, flecked with concern, betrayed his anxiety over the delay.

"Any update on the shipments?" he asked, his voice steady but edged with worry.

One of the dock officials, a young man with a nervous demeanor, shook his head. "We are still tracking its location, Mr. Mehta. It should have been here by now."

"Wasn't it scheduled to arrive by noon?" Achal's brow furrowed.

"There has been a slight delay," the official responded.

"Keep me updated the moment you hear anything. The shipment is crucial." Achal's tone left no room for doubt about the importance of the cargo. Rumors among the dock workers suggested it was an advanced weapon, stirring speculations of imminent conflict.

Capitol High, Mars

High-ranking officials from China, Russia, Brazil, the United States of America, Japan, and Great Britain gathered in a grand hall. The atmosphere was tense, with whispers of a looming threat. Achal entered the room, instantly sensing the gravity of the situation.

A delegate from America was speaking, his voice tinged with skepticism. "Are you sure your intel is trustworthy?"

Mahendra Singh, the Prime Minister of New India on Mars, responded firmly, "Yes, I am sure, Mr. Feder."

"Ah, Mr. Mehta, about time!" the Prime Minister greeted Achal.

"Mr. Prime Minister," Achal nodded.

"Is the shipment here?" the Prime Minister asked.

"Yes, there was a slight delay, but the shipment has been safely received," Achal replied with a sigh of relief. "The ion cannon brought in the shipment is being installed on our best starship as we speak."

"Good," the Prime Minister remarked, turning to the other delegates. "It is about time you all are informed. He continued with a solemn tone "The Domicans are preparing for war. They have assembled a massive fleet with ships far more advanced than anything we possess. We are trying to convince the Terramanes about the violation of the treaty, but we have no evidence, so we must prepare for the worst."

The room erupted into panic, with delegates bombarding the Prime Minister with questions about the threat and its implications for the future of the Earth Federation.

Domican Alpha

"Sir, the fleet is ready and waiting for orders," a Domican officer reported.

The Domicans, standing seven feet tall with six limbs and green skin, were a fearsome sight. The Domicans were once considered savages, but they have made significant progress in their development over the past three centuries. The Domicans were a planet that acted as a catalyst during the Great IntergalaticWar. They harbor deep resentments towards the humans for their humiliating defeat and have been seeking revenge ever since. After the war, they were heavily sanctioned for their war crimes, but now they are prepared to launch an all-out war against humanity. Their leader, the Supreme Commander, addressed his soldiers with a booming voice, "Soldiers, are you all ready?"

"Yes, sire!" the soldiers shouted in unison.

"It is time we take our revenge on those filthy humans for the humiliation they brought to our planet. We will do what our ancestors could not: wipe the humans from the face of the universe. FOR DOMICAN! LONG LIVE THE DOMICAN EMPIRE!"

"For Domican! Long live the empire!" the soldiers echoed, their voices filled with fervor.

Just like the human star system, the Domicans' system had two habitable planets, Domican Alpha and Domican Beta. Until about Seventy years ago, the Domicans were a democracy, but the two fractions held polar opposite ideologies. In 2954 AD, the people of domican Beta, with strong public backing due to the humiliating Treaty of Alkasen. The people of Domican Beta rose and took control, transforming a democracy into an empire. Now, they were fulfilling their promise by preparing for war with humans, who they saw as their sworn enemies.

CHAPTER TWO

CHAPTER 2: SHADOWS OVER MUMBAI

MUMBAI, EARTH

"He won't be able to do it this time."

"I think he'll win again."

The excitement of the speeder race electrified Mumbai, the commercial, fashion, and entertainment capital of India. This city had evolved into the third most important metropolis, trailing only New York and Shanghai. Despite Mars colonization, Earth remained heavily populated with over 15 billion inhabitants, compared to Mars's 2 billion. India was the most populous country, with over 2.5 billion residents, outnumbering Mars's entire population. The discovery of alien life had significantly shifted the political landscape, uniting global governments. Even India, China, and Pakistan had set aside their differences to work together. The Earth Federation, led by India, China, and the United States, comprised Russia, Great Britain, Japan, Australia, France, Brazil, and South Korea. These were the only countries with a presence on Mars. As a superpower, India's Prime Minister, known as the Supreme Minister, represented the Earth Federation in the Council of Planets, an intergalactic peacekeeping body.

Mumbai, characterized by towering skyscrapers with sleek glass exteriors, shimmered in the sunlight. Flying cars zoomed through the air, weaving past vertical gardens and rooftop parks. The city boasted the finest tube transportation system, with self-driving buses and interactive holograms showcasing its technological advancements. Despite congestion, Mumbai's streets, lanes, and homes were powered by sustainable energy sources like wind, solar, water, and hydrogen. While India still held on to its roots and traditions, religion was not widely practiced, but a belief in a higher power responsible for the universe's creation remained.

Speeder racing, a major global sport, captivated audiences on Earth and Mars. These vehicles, resembling bikes, floated five meters above ground and could traverse water and the vertical surfaces of Mumbai's mega-tall towers. The race began at New Nariman Point, a memorial to the old Nariman Point submerged underwater centuries ago. South Mumbai was now underwater, and the race concluded in Borivali, one of the surviving districts from old Mumbai. Speeders, with a maximum speed of 300 km/h, required exceptional control to win.

"There he goes!" "He's in 7th position!"

"Shut up, Avnesh. There's still one round left. He'll catch up," said Anuj, Raj's 15-year-old brother.

Raj Kaushal, a local and fan favorite at 28 years old, stood tall at six feet with a well-built physique, a result of his career as a star pilot for the Indian Air Force. His hazel brown eyes exuded warmth and kindness, reflecting his caring and respectful nature. His curly brown hair added a touch of charm, framing his features with sophistication. Orphaned at 10, Raj raised his brother, who was just six months old at the time, with the help of kind neighbors. Academically bright, Raj was selected for the Air Force straight out of 12th grade and had since become a brilliant star pilot.

Raj zoomed past the 6th and 5th positions in a single turn. With only 9 kilometers left, he overtook the 4th position on a straight road and moved into 3rd place. In the final stretch, Raj trailed the leader, navigating a straight 2-kilometer stretch. The leader tried to block Raj by mirroring his moves. Raj anticipated the tactic and opened the left thrusters to bait the leader. The leader expected Raj to accelerate to the right and followed suit, but Raj flanked left and zoomed past him, winning the race.

"Yes!" cried Anuj in excitement. "Did you all see that? He's, my brother!" Anuj proclaimed proudly. They both love d each other and were proud of everything the other had achieved.

"That was awesome, Dada. How you fooled him at the end was brilliant."

"Thank you, Tam'ma."

"Tam'ma" means younger brother in Kannada. Although not from Karnataka, Raj liked to call his younger brother that.

"In a few years, you'll be able to race too."

"But I won't be as good as you."

"Nonsense," Raj said, dismissing his brother's remark. "You'll be far better than I am."

"You really think so, Dada?"

"Yes, I do."

Just then, Arya, who came in 2nd place, approached Raj. Arya was a friend and fellow pilot. "Congratulations!"

"Thank you, my friend," Raj responded.

"How do you always fool me? You defeated me last year in the last round, and now you've done it again. How is it that I always fall for it?"

"I don't know," Raj said, laughing.

Both friends laughed about it and then went home. Raj lived in Kalyan, a prosperous city and the second largest single district in the country after Thane.

"Dada, can I watch TV?"

"Sure, you can, but only after you finish your homework."

"Fine," Anuj said and left the room.

"Sir, you have mail," said A2NA, the service droid. Droids were common household helpers, with wealthier individuals owning more, symbolizing prosperity.

"Mail!" exclaimed Raj. Mail was not very common and was used only in emergencies, as technology could be hacked.

"What does the mail say, Dada?"

"I've been called to New Delhi. It says there's a chance of war. All personnel have been recalled. The Domicans may attack at any time."

"No, Dada, I won't let you go."

"It's okay, Tam'ma. I'll be back before you know it. Remember what I said: the country always comes first. Besides, I'm sure the war won't happen."

"Okay, Dada. I think you should meet Amayra didi before going."

"Don't get ahead of yourself, little one."

Amayra Mehra was Raj's long-time girlfriend, a top analyst for R.A.W, India's premier spy agency. She had assisted the Air Force and other defense agencies on numerous important missions and assignments.

"Besides, I think she'll be called back too," Raj concluded.

CHAPTER THREE

CHAPTER 3: AMALGAM

DOMICAN ALPHA

The Domicans were fully prepared for battle. Despite some dissent regarding the war, the revolt had been crushed with an iron fist. The Domicans boasted an army of one million—far fewer than the human forces—but their technology was far superior. Their advanced weapons, shields, and stealth technology made them a formidable opponent.

"Sir, the wormhole is ready. Are you sure you want to proceed?"

The high commander, a towering figure with six limbs and green skin, seized the soldier by the neck and growled, "Having second thoughts, soldier?"

"No, sir," the soldier gasped.

"Good. Open the other end of the wormhole at the asteroid belt near Mars and send the army through. The humans shall feel our wrath."

"As you wish, my Lord."

NEW DELHI, EARTH

The military base in New Delhi was one of the largest in the world, located on the outskirts of Delhi NCR. Spanning across seven acres, it was equipped with the latest technology, including self-shield-generating starships and modern Class A-34z fighters. The base also had a space bridge and a strength of about half a million. Soldiers from around the globe, the best of the best, were stationed there. The main hangar was enormous, 22 feet in height and approximately 90,000 square feet, with its own shield generator.

A unique feature of this base was that it was the only one in the world capable of producing combat droids and had a droid army on standby, ready for combat. It was also home to Earth Corps, an elite group of soldiers capable of anything to complete their mission. Their leader, Aryan, was a fearless warrior with a kind heart. Standing over six feet tall, Aryan had a well-defined, muscular body, a chiseled jawline, brown eyes, and long hair. He was almost a knight in shining armor. He carried a specially issued blaster exclusive to Earth Corps. Unlike regular blasters, this one could function as both a rapid blaster, firing 42 shots per minute, and a sniper with a range of 65 meters. Aryan also carried a backup hand blaster, a grenade belt, two hand knives, and a katana. Every member of the Corps was provided with armor capable of withstanding tank-level impacts.

"Wow! It's quite huge," Raj said, marveling at the base.

"You bet. It isn't the biggest base in the world for nothing," replied a fellow soldier.

"By the way, my name is Sam."

"I'm Raj. Where are you from?"

"Australia, mate," Sam replied cheerfully. "I'm a weapons expert."

"I'm a star pilot," Raj said with a proud smile.

"I know. I've heard a lot about you—first in the academy, hero of Operation Altar, and you even collaborated with the Terramanes on a successful mission on Planet Caspban."

"Well, thank you. I didn't realize I was that famous."

MARS

The leaders debated whether the war was truly necessary or if a diplomatic solution could be found. They quickly realized that the Domicans were savages with whom negotiation was impossible.

"Sir, we are mobilizing our army here and on Earth. Our strength on Mars alone far exceeds their army, from what we've heard."

"Never underestimate an enemy. That is the first rule of warfare," said the calm Prime Minister of New India.

"The interplanetary shields and defenses are online and awaiting commands," the Prime Minister's personal assistant reported.

The interplanetary defenses had been developed as the first line of defense in case of war. Shield generators were placed in space to create a protective shield around Earth and Mars at a single command. There were defenses in front of both planets, controlled by a space station in Earth's orbit.

"Achal, how are the weapons coming along?" asked the Prime Minister.

Achal Mehta, a private security provider trusted with national and even global security, was the largest security provider in the world. His family had been in this line of work for a long time, building a strong reputation.

"Well, considering the situation, it's good. Since we're unable to procure weapons from outside due to other systems wanting to remain neutral, the only producers of weapons are humans," Achal said, frustration evident in his voice.

"That's just hypocrisy. How are the Domicans getting their weapons in such quantities?"

"They're using the black market in the Zenex system," Achal explained. Zenex was notorious for its illegal black-market dealings. There was no illegal item you couldn't find there. "We could get weapons from the black market too, but we have these so-called rules that they clearly don't adhere to," Achal said, puzzled by the Prime Minister's adherence to these rules and morals.

"That's what sets us apart from those savages. If we don't follow a set of guidelines, how are we any different from them? Morals make us who we are," the wise Prime Minister responded.

Mahendra Singh was the wisest of the human leaders, embodying all the virtues of a true leader: courage, a kind heart, wisdom, and, most importantly, selflessness. That's why he was elected as the world leader on Mars.

CHAPTER FOUR

CHAPTER 4: CONTACT

NEAR ASTEROID BELT

The Domican fleet emerged from hyperspace just outside the asteroid belt. Their fleet was massive, with the central vessel being the Mothership. This colossal spaceship, dark green in color, was at least five times larger than any ship possessed by humans. It could house an army of around 100,000. The Mothership stood as a behemoth of Domican steel and Lagian glass against the backdrop of the endless cosmos, its sleek metallic surface reflecting the glint of distant stars. It was equipped with 15 standard cannons and four large cannons capable of planetary bombardment. In addition to the Mothership, the fleet included three large Battle Cruisers, each accompanied by two small Star Cruisers and numerous fighter ships.

"High Commander, what are the orders?" asked a subordinate.

"We will wait," the High Commander replied.

"I'm sorry, I don't understand, Commander," the Deputy admitted.

"In two days, they will complete another revolution around their star. Let them celebrate. We will attack when the first rays penetrate the Martian atmosphere. We are well hidden from their scanners. They won't know what hit them," the High Commander said, revealing his personal vendetta against humans. His ancestors had led the Domicans in the 2819 A.D. war, losing all their prestige and respect.

"Very well, Commander. I will brief the army," the Deputy said, still puzzled by the High Commander's strategy.

The Domicans had suffered greatly due to the Treaty of Alkasan after the Intergalactic War. They had been forced to reduce their army strength, grant free hyperspace routes to Earth and other systems through their lanes, and supply Toltarin—a rare mineral native to their system and an excellent power source—to the Earth Federation for a hundred years. This had devastated their economy.

NEW DELHI, EARTH

Soldiers from around the world were assembled at the massive New Delhi base to form a forward strike team. They had amassed a significant arsenal, including nuclear warheads installed in the Destroyer-3, the largest human-made spaceship. This was their primary asset against the Domicans.

"I say we attack first," proposed Aryan, the aggressive leader of Earth Corps. Aryan's leadership style was as fierce as his personality.

Earth Corps boasted a 98% success rate since its founding 100 years ago. Officially an Elite unit in the army, it functioned almost like a separate force with its own Air Force, with the best Star Pilot in the Galaxy and Navy with equally decorated officers to boast of.

"It is not our way," said a man

Raj was present in the meeting, but he did not recognize the man who had just spoken. In truth, he was only physically present, as his mind was elsewhere, captivated by the sight of the Earth Corps training. Joining the Earth Corps as a star pilot had always been his dream.

"We should make it our way," Aryan insisted.

"We have never attacked first in our long history," General Bakshi countered. Raj worked in General Bakshi's unit.

"That's why we've been invaded so many times in our history. Now that I.N.D.I.A is a world leader, we cannot afford to make the same mistakes. This time, not only I.N.D.I.A but the entire world is at stake," Aryan argued.

Raj was part of the Alpha squad, the forward air strike team. They were tasked with welcoming the incoming Domican fleet if the Martian defenses were destroyed. Although the army and resources on Mars were only one-seventh of those on Earth due to its smaller population, Alpha squad's primary mission was to neutralize the Domicans' shields. They had a nuclear warhead and an ion cannon to accomplish this. The ion cannon was mounted on a Venta-class ship called Annihilator-3. Venta-class ships were the only ones capable of carrying both ion cannons and class-one nuclear warheads, designed to initiate uncontrolled chain reactions that could destroy any ship. Once the ion cannon fired, the warhead would be launched after a five-second delay.

MARS

"What caused the war in the first place?" Achal asked.

"It had not been long since we first discovered life outside our system. At that time, the Domicans were not an advanced race. Our war was not with the Domicans specifically but part of a galactic conflict, which we won," the Prime Minister said, sipping his evening tea.

"So, we have no personal vendetta with them?" Achal followed up.

"No, it's just that we were the least advanced race on our side while the Domicans were on theirs. We chose to attack them and emerged victorious, but at a great cost. The Treaty of Alkasan resulted in significant humiliation and financial losses for them. Now they seek retribution," the Prime Minister explained.

"Will the other systems that we fought with help us?"

"They cannot get involved, as it would escalate into a second Intergalactic war," the Prime Minister said.

"But if the Domicans seek revenge, they will attack every system that fought against them."

"Well, systems like Cal-34z, with its galactic capital planet Zander, are too arrogant to admit that the Domicans could defeat them. This arrogance will lead to their downfall," the Prime Minister concluded.

CHAPTER FIVE

CHAPTER 5: THE BEGINNING OF THE END

NEW DELHI, EARTH

The city and the military base were aglow with New Year's Eve celebrations. The base, a beacon of lights, was adorned with festive decorations. People danced and celebrated, oblivious to the looming threat. The city's illumination was so intense that it could be seen from outer space, with fireworks lighting up the sky in vibrant displays.

"It's a great party," remarked Raj, dressed in a tuxedo for the occasion. His discomfort was evident as he repeatedly adjusted his bow tie, which seemed to be choking him.

"Yes, it is," replied Amayra, looking elegant in a red dress. Her long, curled hair and almond-shaped dark brown eyes sparkled under the party lights. Raj found himself mesmerized by her beauty, struggling to find words to express his admiration.

"You look... magnificent tonight," Raj said, pausing to gather his thoughts.

"Thank you," Amayra replied with a smile. "You don't look bad yourself," she added, trying to suppress a laugh at Raj's bow tie troubles.

"I know, but this tie is killing me," Raj complained.

"I wanted to ask you something," Amayra began hesitantly.

"Yes, go ahead," Raj encouraged.

"I wanted to ask... I mean, ah, will—" Amayra's question was interrupted by the blaring emergency alarm.

"What's going on?" Raj asked a fellow soldier, grabbing his arm as people rushed towards the assembly area.

"Mars has been attacked, and we've received a message from the enemy ship."

It was still ten minutes until New Year's on Earth, but Mars had already entered the new year. The Domicans had demolished the planetary defenses on Mars and sent a message to the Earth base.

"What does the message say?"

"It says we have until tomorrow. They will take over Mars by tonight and attack us by tomorrow."

30 MINUTES AGO MARS

"Sir, we have detected movement," a soldier announced.

The Prime Minister rushed into the defense room. On the screen, the massive Domican fleet was approaching Mars.

"My God, they've assembled a fleet beyond imagination," Achal exclaimed, witnessing the enormous fleet.

"Activate the planetary defenses," the Prime Minister ordered, while attempting to contact other leaders through military radio.

At the Prime Minister's command, the planetary shields were raised. A transparent shield enveloped Mars, and the space station was activated, with all satellites set to "kill mode." The planetary defense system, originally designed to stop meteors and asteroids, was now ready to engage with weapons capable of bringing down a spaceship.

"Prepare the Mark-7 and the bomb along with the strike team," the Prime Minister directed. The Mark-7, loaded with an ion cannon shipped by Achal, was a peak example of human engineering.

"Yes, sir," came the response.

As the Domicans approached, all available weapons fired at the forward two ships. The space station also fired its massive blaster, affectionately called the "Mumma." The energized ray struck the ship, creating a thick smoke screen. When the smoke cleared, the ship was unscathed, and the human space station had been destroyed along with the satellites. The shield was now the only defense remaining.

"The strike team is cleared to go."

"Go, go, go!" the leader of the strike team commanded. They were carrying a nuclear warhead in the Mark-7, which, though small compared to the Domican ships, was armed for the mission. Seven fighter ships formed the forward protection, while five others covered the tail.

As they exited the atmosphere, the massive fleet had already breached the defenses.

"Well, boys, let's kick some ass," the leader said.

"Aye, Captain," the pilots responded in unison.

"Sir, the humans have sent some fighters," reported a soldier on the Domican Mothership.

"Send our fighters to intercept them," ordered the Domican Supreme Leader, smirking at the futile efforts of the humans. He thought, "It's cute that humans are putting up a fight, but it's all in vain."

As the human fighters approached the fleet, they were met by a swarm of enemy fighters. The leader of the human strike team ordered his pilots to keep the package safe as they engaged in combat.

A swarm of enemy fighter descended directly upon the Mark-7 and its escort squadron. The human fighters held its attack formation, while the protection tail assumed a defensive posture. Suddenly, the Ship on the leader's starboard side spiraled out of control, colliding with an enemy fighter in a fiery explosion, destroying both. The Control Room lost all visibility as the enemy fighters swarmed the Mark-7. In a desperate maneuver, the strike team unleashed their full arsenal, carving a path through the chaos. What remained of the protective tail regrouped and rejoined the attack formation to facilitate the escape.

"The package is on its way; I repeat, the package is delivered."

"Good job, soldier. Retreat at once."

"Yes, sir."

"Retreat, I repeat, RETREAT!" the leader ordered.

The human ships were falling rapidly. The Mark-7 successfully reached the Domican fleet and locked onto a target.

"Sir, it's locked and loaded."

"FIRE!" screamed the Mark-7 Captain.

The nuclear warhead sped towards its target, and a massive explosion followed. The crew of the Mark-7 and those in the control center cheered, believing they had destroyed the ship.

However, as the smoke cleared, the Domican ship was revealed, still intact with its blue shield glowing brightly. The nuclear warhead strongest ever man-made weapon had failed to penetrate the shield. The crew of Mark-7 looked on in abject terror and horror as the Domican ship powered up its blasters, bracing for the inevitable confrontation. The Mark-7 was soon obliterated by the Domican ship's blaster.

"This is a war we cannot win," remarked the Prime Minister, watching as their hopes disintegrated into space dust.

CHAPTER SIX

CHAPTER 6: FIRST STAND

NEW DELHI

The base in New Delhi was in chaos as the news of Mars's fall reached them. Everyone scrambled to their posts, trying to prepare for the imminent threat.

"Sir, why am I off the team?" Raj asked his Supervising Officer. He had been unexpectedly pulled from the Alpha team and assigned to standby for another mission.

"I need you alive for another mission if our current plans fail. You'll be debriefed in about 30 minutes," the Supervising Officer said hurriedly before rushing off.

The Domicans were advancing towards Earth. The Alpha team was preparing for battle, and the Destroyer-3 was readied for action. Raj, bound by orders, could do nothing but wait.

"Sir, the Planetary Defense is online," reported a technician.

"Good," replied General Bakshi. He was a fair-skinned man of average height, known for his unconventional but effective strategies. Despite the gravity of the situation, he remained composed.

The Domican fleet entered Earth's orbit, and it was evident that the planetary defenses were no match for their advanced technology. The planetary weapons caused minimal damage, only slowing the Domicans down and creating a haze of smoke. The front two Domican ships repositioned to allow the Mothership to fire. A massive cannon, the size of a seven-story building, emerged from the Mothership's forecastle. The ion cannon fired, leaving a trail of destruction as it hit the Space Centre, obliterating it and rendering all defenses offline.

"Sir, the defenses and the station are gone, and they are now coming directly for us," Khan, a Staff Sergeant from the Bangladeshi army, reported.

"Is the Alpha team ready to launch?" General Bakshi shouted, his face showing concern.

"Yes, sir."

"Well, what are you waiting for? Greenlight them!" General Bakshi ordered.

"Sir, Captain Laney is giving a speech," came the response.

"Not again. Tell him we don't have much time," Bakshi said, clearly frustrated.

"My brothers, this is our moment. A moment to shine, to do something that truly matters. We will go out there and fight with everything we have. Maybe you'll meet your fate out there, but you'll die a hero. It's not just for our country, but for all of mankind! So are you with me?" Captain Laney's speech was impassioned.

"YES SIR!" the soldiers responded with fervor.

"Till the end," the soldiers affirmed, pumped up by Laney's words.

"You have to admit, sir, whenever he speaks, it gives you goosebumps," commented one officer.

"That was an inspiring speech, Captain," General Bakshi complimented.

"Thank you, sir!" replied Captain Laney.

"So, you and your men are ready?" Bakshi asked.

"Sir, we were born ready," Laney affirmed.

"Good. Your mission is a go," Bakshi said.

"All right, boys, let's go. Chop chop!" Laney ordered his squadron.

The Alpha team and Destroyer-3 were prepared for battle after Laney's motivating speech. Alpha squadron flew into the air, with Destroyer-3 at its center in a tight formation. As they crossed the mesosphere, the Domican fleet came into view, though two ships were missing from the initial sighting. The Domicans had left a quarter of their fleet on Mars to suppress any resistance. Despite this, their remaining fleet was still formidable.

MARS

Mars was now entirely under Domican control. The once-majestic cities were reduced to ruins. The new Qutb Minar, the tallest building in the solar system, had been reduced to ashes. The important cities and military bases were destroyed, leaving no room for human resistance.

The leaders and surviving civilians had taken refuge in an underground nuclear bunker. Half of the population had been evacuated to a base on the Moon, which was equipped with anti-gravity weapons for defense.

"What should we do now, sir?" asked the Deputy of Security for the Prime Minister.

"We need to plan a counterattack," the Prime Minister responded, though the human forces on Mars were outnumbered and technologically inferior, making any counterattack nearly impossible.

EARTH

The Alpha Squad was nearing the Domican fleet with Destroyer-3 ready to deploy its nuclear bomb. Alpha leader was positioned at the north of the Destroyer. The Domican Wingers, intent on destruction, were closing in. The Alpha team prepared for the onslaught. The Wingers attacked the forward formation, and A-1 and A-4 narrowly escaped ion blasts, but A-3 was overwhelmed and went down. The backward wings broke formation to attack, and A-7, pursued by three Wingers, but he was a witty pilot so he turned on the reserve blasters and thrusters causing a back thrust of the wings. As he went up and above the 3 wingers, they saw in disbelieve. A-7 was now behind the wingers and locked on the targets and blasted them to hell.

"Boys, we need to deliver the package," Laney said with urgency. "It's now or never."

The Alpha squad was being decimated. Laney, witnessing the loss of his men, struggled to maintain focus. Despite his brilliant strategizing, his thoughts were clouded by the loss of his squad.

"Alpha leader, come in," Prash (A-7) called. When there was no response, he urged, "Sir, get yourself together. This is not the time to dwell on the past. We need you. You're our best hope. Snap out of it; we have a battle to win."

Laney shook off his despair and turned his ship around. "Thank you, soldier."

"Anytime, sir. But we still need a plan."

"I already have one." Laney switched to an open channel. "All Alphas, form up on me. Is the Destroyer still intact?"

"Yes, sir," came the reply from the commanding officer of Destroyer-3.

Raj had just been briefed about his mission. His task was to travel to Planet Zander and seek help from the council of planets, as well as procure a powerful ship rumored to exist in the black market of Zander. This ship was said to be capable of destroying a Class-A1 Cruiser and outrunning any vessel in the galaxy.

"So, this charade is just a distraction?" Raj asked.

"Yes, it's their mission to clear a path for you," replied General Bakshi. "Your mission is thc onc that truly matters."

"It's suicide," Raj protested. "Do they know about it?"

"Yes, they do. In fact, they volunteered for the mission."

"This ship you speak of—does it even exist, or is it just an urban legend?"

"No one knows, but it's our best hope."

"So, you're risking countless lives on a legend?"

"Raj, you're young and may not understand this now, but everything depends on hope. Hope is what drives us. It's what gets us up every morning, hoping for a better day. When the time comes, you'll understand."

Alpha squad was still trapped amidst waves of enemy fighters.

"Boys we are going with Flamingo" ordered Laney to his fighters

"But captain"

"No buts, it's our only way out"

The squadron formed up on their leader for the risky Flamingo maneuver, a last-ditch, high-risk strategy. The remaining fighters grouped around the Destroyer-3, ready for the plan.

On the base, Raj prepared for his mission. General Bakshi introduced Raj's team, which included a co-pilot, combatants, a marksman, a tech support, and a skilled sergeant.

"Raj, you'll lead a team of five people, a battle droid, and a techno droid. This is Aaron, your co-pilot. This is Tanvi, a hand-to-hand combatant. Next is Anuraag, an exceptional marksman. Arnav will handle tech support. Lastly, this is James, a capable warrior and your second-in-command," Bakshi introduced.

As Raj greeted his team, Aryan, the leader of the Earth corps, arrived.

"Sir, they need to leave now. Captain Laney is initiating the Flamingo maneuver, which will give them a brief window to pass through the enemy blockade."

"FLAMINGO!" Raj exclaimed. "That's a suicide mission. General, you must stop them; they'll get themselves killed."

The Alpha Squad is nearing the enemy ships as the fighters prepare. All remaining Alpha fighters formed a V-formation around the Destroyer-3, creating a shield to protect the package.

Despite his reservation about the plan, Raj was prepared to lead his team on the critical mission to Zander. His team was set to depart aboard the Phantom, a Class-3 fighter vessel one of the few man-made Ships capable of hyperspace travel and equipped with ray-shield. All necessary supplies for the mission had been loaded on the Ship and the crew was ready to leave.

"Raj, you need to be in position and ready for Laney's signal. The Alpha Squad will create a narrow window for your escape, so you must be ready. The fate of two worlds rests on your mission's success. There is no room for error. Farewell, and godspeed," the General concluded.

"A-3 and A-7, on me," Laney ordered his fighters as he led them into battle. Laney shot down two enemy fighters in a fierce dogfight. A-7, after a close battle with an enemy fighter, emerged victorious. Two more fighters fell, leaving only five. Destroyer-3, with its powerful weapon, moved forward, shooting down any craft in its path.

"Captain, we need to press right now; we've cleared a path for the Destroyer," a squad member said.

"Alright, I'll get the word to Phantom," Laney responded.

"Alpha leader to Phantom, Alpha leader to Phantom."

"Go ahead, Alpha leader. This is pack leader Raj."

"Ah, my friend it's good to hear your voice,"

"Likewise, old friend," Raj replied.

"You have one shot at this. The Destroyer will fire its nuclear warhead at the enemy Mothership. I don't know if it will penetrate, but it will create chaos. That's when you need to escape."

Raj sighed, knowing the gravity of the situation. "I understand. Be careful," he said, showing concern.

"Ain't I always?" Laney replied with a smile, though he knew the mission was likely a one-way trip.

Destroyer-3 accelerated toward the Mothership, deflecting enemy attacks with its ray shields. Laney and his squadron pressed forward. A-3 was hit and, with his left thrusters damaged, chose to make a final sacrifice, taking out numerous enemy fighters before his ship exploded.

"Goodbye, soldier. Your sacrifice will not be in vain," Laney said, as he continued toward the Mothership.

CHAPTER SEVEN

CHAPTER 7: INTO THE FRAY

The Moon base, shrouded in secrecy and advanced cloaking, was a refuge for Mars's civilians. The southernmost pole, known as the Darkside, provided perfect concealment. It was a well-equipped sanctuary, prepared to endure a prolonged conflict with its sophisticated defenses and cloaking systems.

As the base remained hidden from enemy radar, the civilian and military personnel within braced themselves for a potentially long stay. The atmosphere was tense but hopeful; they knew their survival depended on the successful execution of the mission on Earth.

MARS

On Mars, the remaining forces had consolidated their efforts to plan a counterattack. The situation was grim.

"Sir, a counterattack will be very difficult," the Military General of New India reported, his tone laden with pessimism. "The Domicans have doubled their patrols. We have little ammunition left and our troops are in poor condition."

"But we have to do something," insisted another officer.

"I think our best option right now is to hope that our forces on Earth have more success than we do," the General continued.

"We can't just sit here and do nothing," another officer argued.

"We will strike back, sir. Believe me, we will. But we have to wait until the major Domican force attacking Earth is weakened. Only then can we strike with our full might and reclaim our planet."

"I hope you're right, General," the commander replied, resigned but hopeful.

OUTER ATMOSPHERE, EARTH

In the outer atmosphere, Laney and his squadron were preparing for the final assault.

"Laney, we're ready and waiting for your signal," Raj reported, his voice steady despite the tension.

"Your moment will be soon, Raj," Laney replied, guiding his fighters closer to the Mothership.

"Captain, we need to clear the strike point," a squad member suggested.

"I agree," Laney said, maneuvering through enemy lines. "We'll wait until the moment is right."

The Stran-1 fighters, tasked with defending the Mothership, formed a formidable barrier. Laney and his wingman knew the risks involved in using their ion cannons, but it was their only option.

"Captain, I'm ready and awaiting your order," said the wingman.

"Not yet," Laney said, his eyes fixed on the enemy formations. "Not now."

"Anytime, Captain."

"Wait," Laney commanded, as they closed in on the target. "Now!"

With a decisive command, Laney and his wingman unleashed their ion cannons. The blasts tore through the enemy ranks, creating a massive explosion that sent the remaining fighters into chaos.

"Now is the time to drop the big boy," Laney instructed. "Raj, be ready to leave. It's time."

"Copy, Captain," Raj responded, bracing for the crucial moment.

The Captain of Destroyer-3 issued his final command. "Fire!" The nuclear warhead was launched toward the Mothership, creating a blinding explosion that illuminated the night sky as if it were day.

"Raj, leave now before the smoke clears," Laney urged.

"Aaron, are the coordinates encoded and the hyperdrive prepped?" Raj asked.

"Yes, Captain," Aaron confirmed.

"Good. Make the jump."

Laney's voice, tinged with emotion, reached Raj. "Remember, I'll always be with you even if I'm not there."

"I know, brother. To infinity and beyond. Right?" Raj recalled their pact, a promise made long ago.

"Yes, always."

"I'll see you soon."

"I hope not," Laney said with a bittersweet smile, knowing his fate.

As Laney's fighter was struck by a photon blast, it was destroyed instantly, taking the rest of Alpha Squad with it.

"NOOOO!" Raj cried out as Phantom, his fighter, entered hyperspace, leaving behind the devastation and the memory of his fallen comrades.

Raj's journey to Planet Zander was perilous and fraught with danger. Despite the pain of losing his friends, he knew that the mission was more important than ever. As Phantom hurtled through hyperspace, Raj steeled himself for the challenges ahead.

On Planet Zander, Raj and his team would face new adversaries and unexpected allies in their quest to find the legendary ship that could turn the tide of the war. The battle for Earth and Mars was far from over, and Raj's determination burned brighter than ever, fueled by the memory of those who had sacrificed everything for the mission's success.

With the fate of humanity resting on their shoulders, Raj and his team prepared to navigate the treacherous underworld of Zander, where the line between friend and foe was as thin as a razor's edge. Their journey was just beginning, and the stakes had never been higher.

CHAPTER EIGHT

CHAPTER 8: ZANDAR

HYPERSPACE

Raj's destination, Planet Zander, was known for its underground markets and the elusive council of planets. It was a place where the laws of the galaxy were bent, if not entirely ignored. The journey was perilous, but Raj and his team were determined.

The Phantom sped through hyperspace, a realm of swirling colors and impossible geometries that defied conventional understanding. Unlike popular belief, hyperspace wasn't a tunnel but a shortcut, a faster route through the cosmos. Inside the ship, the crew debated how best to support their captain, Raj, who had isolated himself since their entry into hyperspace.

"Should we say something to him?" one crewmate asked.

"I think he needs to be left alone for a while," another replied.

As they spoke, Raj emerged from his quarters. "Are we there yet, Aaron?" he asked, his voice steady despite his visible fatigue.

"Almost, sir," Aaron responded.

"Good. Take the ship out of hyperspace once we're near the rings of Zander."

"Yes, Captain."

"We need to be prepared for anything. This mission is our only hope," Raj said.

As Phantom sped through hyperspace, Raj gathered his team for a briefing. They discussed strategies, potential threats, and the elusive ship they were tasked to find. The tension was palpable, but so was the resolve.

EARTH

The Domicans, having crushed the Earth's air force, now pressed their ground assault. Their mothership continued to function as a command center from the outer atmosphere, while two star cruisers landed in the Indian and Pacific Oceans. The United Naval Forces tried in vain to halt the Domican invasion but were overwhelmed.

The Domican soldiers, equipped with ray shield armor, made their way to land in small starships. Their advanced armor rendered human weapons ineffective.

"Why can't we kill them?" demanded the Defence Secretary of India.

"Sir, their ray shields render our weapons useless," Aryan, the leader of Earth Corps, explained.

"Ray shields on such a small scale? I thought that technology was still far off," the Defence Secretary replied.

"It appears they've achieved it," Aryan confirmed.

"Is there any weakness in these ray armors?"

"Our research team is working hard to find one, but so far, they haven't had any luck," Aryan said.

"Redirect all research personnel to this task. It's our top priority."

"Yes, sir."

Hyperspace

"Sir, we're almost there," Aaron reported as they approached the massive rings of Zander.

"Very well. Revert the controls to me. I'll take us out."

"Everyone, stay sharp. We don't know what we're walking into," Raj warned.

"Yes, sir."

The Phantom emerged from hyperspace just before the rings. The crew gazed in awe at the vast, glittering rings encircling the planet. They seemed to be made of some unknown material.

"The rings appear to be made of debris," Arnav, the tech specialist, observed.

"Looks organic to me," Tanvi countered.

"Alright, we're approaching the planet," Raj announced.

"Sir, we're low on fuel," Aaron said.

"Turn off the thrusters immediately," Raj ordered.

"Yes, sir."

"James, reroute the auxiliary power to the main engines."

"I'm on it," James replied.

"Arnav, turn on the deflectors."

"Yes, Captain."

"Brace yourselves. We're going for a spin."

As the Phantom entered Zander's atmosphere, the auxiliary power dwindled. The ship plummeted rapidly due to gravity.

"Sir, we're officially out of power. The only thing driving us is gravity!" Aaron reported, panic evident in his voice.

"We'll use gravity to our advantage. We only need to land in one piece, not fly. We can still do that," Raj assured.

"And how did the fuel run out on such an important mission?" Raj wondered aloud.

"Sir, I filled the fuel to capacity. It could only hold this much," Aaron explained.

"Brilliant. Nonetheless, let's focus on landing."

The Phantom descended like a shooting star.

"Sir, we're 100 meters from the ground," Aaron said, his voice tight with fear.

"James, is there any reserved power for the lights? Reroute it to the engines. You'll need to override the controls."

"Yes, Captain."

"What's your plan, Captain?" Arnav asked.

"If we can get enough power, we can use the engines for back thrust to counteract gravity," Raj explained.

"Sir, I'm ready to turn on the power," James said.

"Do it on my mark."

"Sir, we're 40 meters away."

"I know."

"30 meters."

"Not yet."

"20 meters."

"Wait."

"10 meters!"

"Now!"

The reserved power activated the engines just in time. The Phantom back-thrusted, reducing the impact as it hit the ground. It still landed heavily but with less force.

"I think that went as planned," Raj said with a slight smirk. The crew, though relieved, was visibly shaken by the landing.

"Alright, we need to move swiftly if we're to get back in time. Gather what you need from the stronghold. I'll be there shortly."

"Is there something you need to do, Captain?" Arnav asked.

"I need to hail the command center and report our successful touchdown on Zander."

"Okay, Captain."

Raj contacted the command center in New Delhi. "Do you read me, General?"

"Loud and clear, Captain. Proceed."

"Sir, we've successfully reached Zander. We're currently on the outskirts of the planet-city."

"Well done, Raj. Find the ship quickly and return home. We're on a tight schedule."

"Yes, sir."

As they landed, Raj couldn't help but think of the sacrifices made by the Alpha team. The weight of their mission pressed heavily on his shoulders, but failure was not an option. The fate of Earth and Mars depended on their success. The team's mission was clear: find the council, secure the ship, and return to aid in the battle against the Domicans.

"Welcome to Zander. Let's move," Raj ordered, as the team disembarked, ready to face whatever challenges awaited them.

The mission was far from over, but Raj and his team were determined to see it through, no matter the cost. The hope of two worlds rested on their shoulders, and they would not let it falter.

With Raj and his team embarking on their perilous mission, the stage is set for a thrilling confrontation on Planet Zander. The stakes are higher than ever, and the resolve of our heroes will be tested to the fullest. The battle for Earth and Mars continues, with the fate of humanity hanging in the balance.

Earth

The Domican armor's advanced technology continued to outmatch human defenses. With their landing in Delhi, the Earth Corps were deployed to defend the city. A complete lockdown was enforced, transforming Delhi into a fortress.

"What's the status of the Corps?" General Bakshi inquired.

"Sir, we've engaged the Domicans and are actively fighting them," Aryan reported.

The Domicans had landed their ship on the outskirts of Delhi, destroying a settlement that was fortunately unoccupied as civilians had been evacuated to a massive bunker.

"Sir, we've moved most civilians to the bunker, but some are still in the line of fire and could not be evacuated in time," Captain Rathod, the Deputy of General Bakshi, reported in his heavy South Indian accent.

"Send a rescue team to get those civilians to safety."

"Yes, sir."

Meanwhile, analysts were working tirelessly to find a weakness in the Domican armor.

"The armor appears to be centrally powered," said Amayra, now the chief analyst. "Locating the power unit is crucial."

"So, where do you think the generator might be?" General Bakshi asked, his tone tense.

"Probably on the starship that landed in Delhi," Amayra suggested.

"So, if we manage to destroy a kilometer-long starship outside our city without decimating Delhi, they'll be defenseless?" General Bakshi asked skeptically.

"We're not certain yet. We need more time for confirmation."

"Keep me informed as soon as you know."

"Yes, sir."

Back on Zander, Raj and his team ventured towards the planet-city's stronghold, their mission clear and their resolve unwavering. The battle for humanity's survival was far from over, and every decision they made would shape the fate of their world.

CHAPTER NINE

CHAPTER 9: THE SEARCH FOR THE RAVEN

The sun rose over the city-planet of Zander, casting a warm, golden hue across its landscape. For its inhabitants, the sunrise symbolized hope and renewal. Yet, on Earth, the same celestial event brought only the grim reminder of a daily struggle for survival. As humanity grappled with despair, the fight to reclaim their world seemed increasingly futile.

ZANDER

Raj and his team, now deep within the labyrinthine underworld of Zander, continued their search for the legendary ship. Despite their efforts, they had uncovered nothing concrete—only whispers and legends. The hope of finding the ship, their last hope, seemed to be slipping away with each passing moment.

A sudden voice broke the silence, startling the team. They turned to find a towering figure standing behind them—an imposing, eight-foot-tall being with green skin, crimson eyes, and a physique that was both human and alien.

"I heard you're looking for a ship," the figure said, his voice echoing with an almost mystical quality.

Raj, cautious but intrigued, asked, "Who told you?"

"Well, how many people wander the underworld in search of a legendary ship?" the green man replied. "Actually, many do, but not everyone is seeking the Raven."

"The what?" Raj responded; his disbelief evident.

"The Raven," the green man repeated. "It's the ship you're after—faster than light, capable of destroying any vessel in the blink of an eye. Ring any bells?"

Raj was taken aback. "What do you know about it?"

As Raj, Arnav, and Tanvi struggled to comprehend the situation, the rest of the team was engaged in a crucial task. Aaron, James, and Anuraag were attempting to persuade the Council of Planets to intervene in the conflict with the Domicans. The council, composed of sixteen members, required a majority of ten votes to take action.

The green man continued, "I don't know much, but I can lead you to it."

"And you'll tell us?" Raj asked, weighing the risk of trusting this enigmatic figure.

"For the right price," the green man replied. "It'll depend on how important it is to you."

"It's crucial—not just for us but for our entire race. We're under attack by the Domicans, and we need the ship to save our civilization."

The mention of the Domicans caused the green man to pause. "The Domicans?" he asked, his tone shifting abruptly.

"Yes, the Domicans," Raj confirmed.

The green man's demeanor changed from casual to serious. "Alright, I'll take you to the ship."

"Why the sudden change?" Tanvi asked, her suspicion evident.

"Do you want the ship or not?" the green man snapped, his patience wearing thin.

"Yes, we do!" Raj's voice was unusually firm, revealing the gravity of their situation.

The other team members were still in the midst of their high-stakes negotiation with the council. Aaron, James, and Anuraag presented all their evidence, hoping to convince the council to act quickly. They waited anxiously for a decision, knowing that the fate of Earth hinged on the council's response.

Meanwhile, the green man led Raj and his team to a seemingly abandoned hangar in the underworld. The structure appeared derelict from the outside, leading Raj to question its credibility.

"Are you sure this is the right place?" Raj asked, his skepticism evident.

"Trust me, the ship is here," the green man assured, attempting to calm Raj's growing doubts. Yet, the questions persisted: Who was this mysterious figure? Why was he helping them? What was his motive? Most pressing of all, how could they trust a stranger with the future of their civilization hanging in the balance?

As Raj and his team prepared to enter the hangar, the tension was palpable. The fate of their mission—and perhaps the future of Earth—depended on the truth of the green man's claims and the success of their quest.

CHAPTER TEN

CHAPTER 10: THE BREAKTHROUGH

EARTH

It had been six days since the Domicans landed on Earth, and their resistance had been fiercer than anticipated. With civilians relocated to underground bunkers and world forces battling desperately, the situation was dire. Engineers, scientists, and soldiers worked around the clock to find a weakness in the Domican armor. Finally, a breakthrough came.

"SIR, I've found a weakness!" Amayra burst into the control room; her eyes wide with excitement. As the chief of the technical department, she had been relentless in her search for a solution. Her announcement drew immediate attention from everyone in the room.

"GOD BLESS YOU, AMAYRA!" General Bakshi exclaimed; his relief palpable. "Please, explain."

Amayra took a deep breath. ""Yes Sir, as most of you know that a deflector on such a small scale is next to impossible. But the Domicans, found a way. We discovered that the Domicans are powering their ray shields remotely. They've set up devices near every major city—each one is crucial for their armor's functionality. We've pinpointed a device that matches the frequency of their armor. We need to destroy it."

"Sounds promising, but how do we infiltrate the Command Ships with their ray shields?" General Bakshi asked, his face creased with concern.

"The device powering the ray shields shuts off or reloads every 12 hours for exactly 110 seconds," Amayra explained. "We need to strike during that window."

"That's a tight window," Bakshi mused. "But what choice do we have?"

Amayra nodded. "It's our best shot."

Bakshi paced the room, considering the options. "Alright, we have two days to plan and execute this before it's too late. We'll organize into three teams: The first team will be the support team, led by me and Amayra. The second team will distract the Domican guards away from the Mothership. The third team, the strike team, will be the Earth Corps elite forces led by Aryan. Any questions?"

"No, General," came the unified response from the room, their morale lifted by the new strategy.

"Disseminate this plan to all stations worldwide," Bakshi ordered. "Also, get me an update on the Earth Corps' rescue mission."

"Yes, sir," Aryan replied via hologram. "The mission was successful, but we lost many good men."

"I'm sorry for your loss," Bakshi said somberly. "Their sacrifice will not be in vain. We must honor their memory by winning this battle. Return to base; we now have a chance."

Fortunes appeared to be turning in humanity's favor,as they discovered a critical weakness that could cripple the Dominican's terrestrial army. Meanwhile, on Zander Raj's team had achieved the success on both the front by locating the ship capable of breaching Domican defense, additionally, the Council of Planets have ruled in Earth's favor, pleading to send reinforcements to assist in the war efforts.

ZANDER

Back on Zander, Raj and his team finally located the legendary ship, a vessel of awe-inspiring design. The ship was a deep, hot red—its armor seemed forged in the heart of a supernova, with weaponry that looked otherworldly.

"It's magnificent," Raj said, gazing at the ship in admiration.

"It's a work of art," Arnav added, his voice filled with reverence.

The green man revealed, "It's called Lucifer."

"Lucifer, like the devil from Christian mythology?" Arnav asked, his curiosity piqued.

"Yes, because the creator of this ship was human," the green man confirmed.

"A human?" Raj, Arnav, and Tanvi exclaimed in unison.

"Yes," the green man said, his tone tinged with nostalgia. "Mark, the ship's creator, was a dear friend of mine."

Raj, overwhelmed with questions, asked, "What? How? When? Most importantly, WHO?"

"I thought you were short on time," the green man responded, his patience wearing thin.

"Yes, we are," Raj replied urgently.

"Then just take the ship and go before I change my mind," the green man said, his voice softening.

"Arnav, prep the systems and the engine," Raj commanded.

"On it, Captain," Arnav responded, heading to the controls.

Raj, noticing the green man's distress, asked, "Why are you helping us?"

"Because Mark would have wanted this," the green man said, his voice quivering with emotion. "He and my family were all lost when the Domicans attacked my planet, Alyx-2. We were isolated, far off the intergalactic routes. No one came to our aid. Mark was visiting with me when it happened."

"I'm so sorry for your loss," Raj said, placing a comforting hand on the green man's shoulder.

"Just make sure your planet doesn't suffer the same fate," the green man said, his eyes reflecting both sorrow and hope.

"I promise we will fight with everything we have," Raj assured him.

With the ship prepared and the alliance of the Council of Planets secured, Raj and his team were ready to return to Earth. The Lucifer was their beacon of hope, and the time to act was now. As they prepared for their departure, the weight of their mission settled heavily on their shoulders. The fate of Earth depended on their success, and they were determined to see it through to the end.

CHAPTER ELEVEN

CHAPTER 11: THE TURNING POINT

EARTH

The war on Earth has intensified, as humanity now posessessed a viable strategy. The intelligence from the Delhi base has proved crucial. In Delhi, the plan was on the verge of extinction as the two teams approached the Domican's command ship.

"We are in position", Aryan communicated through the hologram." We need that distraction immediately!"

The second team's leader responded," prepare to advance, the distraction is imminent".

As, Harry, the commander of the second team, finished speaking, a specialized customized G-9 class armored vehicle roared onto the scene, its weapon blazing.

The advanced truck, towering at 10 feet height and eight feet wide, was equipped with a Gatling gun atop and four iron blasters- two on either side. The Gatling gun fired energy charges rather than bullets, creating a barrage that felt as though it was raining fire.

"That's one way to do it" Aryan remarked.

"This is the vanguard" Harry noted "You've got about 10 minutes at most. Move swiftly".

"Alright, everyone. They're risking their life to buy us this opportunity. We have one chance, so let's make it count."

"Yes, Captain!" the soldiers responded in unison.

"Bole So Nihal...Sat Sri Akaal" shouted Aryan, his voice echoing with the timeless Punjabi war cry. The soldiers joined in unison, their voices reverberating: "BOLE SO NIHAL...SAT SRI AKAAL". The intensity of their shout was so powerful it almost silenced their surroundings.

. "According to the intelligence provided, the power generator will shut down in exactly three minutes. Once it does, we'll have just 110 seconds to destroy it. We can't afford any mistakes. let's move!" Aryan commanded.

The strike team infiltrated the Ship through the service ducts. "Sir, the hallway is clear" one solider reported. "Move in," Aryan ordered. As they emerged into the open, the Domicans alerted by the alarm, began to engage them.

"How many do you see?" Aryan asked, firing at the enemy.

"I've got eight targets," replied one solider. "I see nine more" another confirmed.

"New plan," Aryan said decisively. "Five of you will engage the enemy here. The renaming three will come with me. We'll take an alternate route to disarm the generator. Omn my count- throw smokes"

Under the cover of the heavy smoke, Aryan and his team raced towards the corridor ahead. Just round the corner, they spotted a service duct. They crawled through it, emerging on the other side of the Ship, just a passage away from the generator.

"That was easier than expected. How much time before the generator goes offline?" Aryan inquired.

"Sir, we've got about a minute "came the reply.

The team breached the blast doors with ease, only to discover additionally security inside the chamber they did not account for. The generator was encased in a steel-like material that they hadn't anticipated.

"Sir, this wasn't part of the plan," one solider noted.

"We'll improvise," Aryan responded, inspecting the enclosure. Unable to determine what it is made of, he ordered, "Plant explosive around it"

Time was running out. The generator was about to shut down, and once it did, they would have just 110 seconds to destroy it before it would automatically reactivate. The team planted the explosives and retreated to a safe distance. The explosion shook the air with a tremendous bang. As the smoke cleared, they moved in to assess the damage.

"Sir, the enclosure is still intact, though slightly damaged."

"what's the next move?" the team asked.

"We now know it can be destroyed," Aryan said " We need to take a risk and use one of the ray bombs."

"But sir, we need those for the generator," a solider objected.

"How many do we have?" Aryan asked.

"Sir three" came the response.

"We'll use one. I believe two will be enough to take out the generator. Plant the first one where the encloser is weakest," Aryan ordered after inspecting the structure again. "Right here, in the center". The team planted the ray bomb on the designated spot and armed it.

"Do we start the countdown? The generator goes offline in less than ten seconds," a solider asked.

"By all means, proceed," Aryan replied.

The bomb detonated with such force that the noise nearly shattered the sound barrier. The team rushed forward to check if the blast had succeeded in breaching the enclosure.

"Yessss" one solider exclaimed as they saw a hole had been blown into the container.

"We're not finished yet," Aryan reminded them. "How much time do we have?"

"Sir the generator went offline about ten seconds ago, we have less than 100 seconds before it reactivates"

"Quickly, roll the bombs slowly towards the generator as we cannot go near it due to the radiation," Aryan commanded.

The generator radiated rays of an unknown energy, likely stemming from its power source material. This radiation, harmful to humans but not to the Domicans, posed a significant threat. Aryan and his team carefully rolled the ray bombs towards the generator with so much precision that it stopped right at the foot of the generator.

"Start the countdown," Aryan ordered. The team sprinted off the ship, knowing the impending explosion would obliterate everything.

"Charlie to Tango, Charlie to Tango do you copy?" Aryan called out through his hologram.

"Yes, we copy" responded the Tango leader.

"Get all of the men off the Ship, we have initiated the countdown. We have about 30 seconds left" Aryan commanded.

"Right away, Charlie leader" came the prompt reply.

The corps deployed half a dozen smoke grenades, covering the entire ship in a thick cloud. The smoke blinded the Domicans along with the ship's defense system. As the stopwatch hit zero, the team had already eacaped, running as far s possible from the vessel. Expecting a colossal explosion, they glanced back, only to witness something far more unexpected-the generator didn't explode with a bang. Instead, it collapsed into a singularity, absorbing the ship and everything around it. Like a snake devouring its own tail, the entire structure was consumed in a violent implosion, leaving behind a flash of light and a deafening burst of sound.

"That was a beautiful sight to witness, not gonna lie," one of the corps remarked.

"I'd agree" replied Aryan

"Sir, the mission is a success! I repeat the mission is a success" Aryan hailed the base, informing them of the operation's outcome. The moment the message reached the base, an eruption of joy and exhilaration spread among everyone-be it Captain, Major, IT personnel, or even General Bakshi himself.

General Bakshi, regaining his composure, gave the final command: "Get this message to all stations and Mars as well. Let them know -the plan is a go!"

With the generator destroyed and the Domican defenses crippled, Earth's forces saw a glimmer of hope. The brilliant explosion had not only dismantled the Domican Command Ship but had also sent a powerful message to both the enemy and Earth's allies. The battle for survival was far from over, but this victory was a critical turning point.

The aftermath of the explosion revealed the scope of the devastation. The once formidable Command Ship had been reduced to debris, the remnants of which were scattered across the battlefield. The shockwave had sent ripples through the surrounding area, but the real victory was the incapacitation of the Domican forces that had been utilizing the Command Ship.

Aryan and his team regrouped, their faces etched with exhaustion and relief. "Well done, everyone," Aryan said, his voice filled with pride. "We've done our part. Now, let's get back to base and prepare for the next phase."

The strike team, still awestruck by the scale of their accomplishment, moved swiftly to extract themselves from the battlefield. Smoke continued to billow from the wreckage as they made their way back to the designated extraction point.

ZANDER

Meanwhile, on Zander, the atmosphere was charged with anticipation. Raj and his team had successfully secured the legendary ship, Lucifer. The ship's power and its potential to turn the tide in the battle against the Domicans were unparalleled.

Raj stood by the ship's control panel, the hum of the powerful engines resonating through the chamber. "We're ready," he said, glancing at Arnav and Tanvi. "Let's get this ship operational and head back to Earth."

Tanvi nodded, her fingers flying over the control panel as she initiated the ship's systems. "All systems are coming online," she reported. "We're good to go."

As the ship powered up, the green man, who had been a crucial ally, approached Raj. "You have the ship now," he said, his voice heavy with emotion. "Please, make sure it's used to its fullest potential. It's our last hope."

"We will," Raj assured him. "Thank you for everything. We'll honor Mark's legacy."

With the ship fully operational, Raj and his team prepared for their journey back to Earth. The Lucifer was a marvel of technology and weaponry, its design a testament to the ingenuity of its creator. As they boarded the ship and set their course for Earth, a new sense of determination filled the crew.

THE FINAL ASSAULT

Back on Earth, the allied forces were preparing themselves for the final assault on the remaining Domican forces. The intelligence gathered from the now-destroyed Command Ship had provided valuable insights into the Domican operations and vulnerabilities. General Bakshi and his team were coordinating the global response, ensuring that every resource was mobilized.

"General Bakshi, we've received word from the strike team," reported an aide. "The mission was a success, and the Domican defenses have been severely compromised."

Bakshi's eyes narrowed with focus. "Excellent. Let's leverage this momentum. Mobilize all available forces. We need to hit the remaining Domican positions hard and fast."

The world's military and defense forces, galvanized by the recent victory, moved into action. The unified efforts of nations and their armies, combined with the newfound advantage of the Lucifer, set the stage for a decisive confrontation.

As the final preparations were underway, Raj and his team in the Lucifer approached Earth's orbit. The sight of the planet, scarred but still vibrant, filled them with a renewed sense of purpose.

"Prepare for atmospheric entry," Raj commanded, his voice steady. "We're going to make sure Earth has a fighting chance."

The Lucifer descended through the atmosphere, its powerful engines blazing through the sky. Below, Earth's defenders prepared to make their stand, their resolve unwavering in the face of the Domican threat.

As the Lucifer landed and its crew disembarked, they were met with cheers and gratitude from the beleaguered forces. Raj, Arnav, Tanvi, and the rest of the team knew that their arrival marked the beginning of a critical phase in the battle for Earth's survival.

The final assault had begun, and with it came the hope of liberation. The fate of Earth hung in the balance, but with the combined strength of humanity and the advanced technology of Lucifer, the tide of war was about to change.

CHAPTER TWELVE

CHAPTER 12: THE FINAL STAND

MARS

The once-bustling Martian colonies were now mostly empty, their populations relocated to the Moon or hidden away in underground bunkers. Mars had become a ghost planet, awaiting any news from Earth that might guide its next steps. The Martian government was in a tense state of anticipation.

"Sir, we have news from Earth," the Secretary General announced to Prime Minister Mahendra Singh.

"What is it?" Singh asked, his voice betraying a mix of hope and apprehension.

"We've received a plan of action to disable the Domican ray shields," the Secretary General replied.

Mahendra Singh's face brightened with a mix of relief and exhilaration. "God bless you!" he shouted, his voice echoing through the chamber. "Inform all personnel and mobilize every resource we have. We need to make sure these invaders are vanquished once and for all!"

EARTH

The war on Earth had reached a critical juncture. The strategy devised by humanity was having a profound impact, with Domican forces in retreat. However, the atmosphere aboard the Domican Command Ship was fraught with tension.

"Sir, humans have identified a flaw in our designs. Our forces are retreating," reported the Domican second-in-command.

"I wanted to rule Earth, to make humans our slaves," the High Commander roared, his voice reverberating with anger. The force of his fury dented the throne he occupied. "Prepare the Equalizer and wait for my command. We shall unleash what they call hellfire upon them!"

The Equalizer was a devastating planetary bombardment weapon capable of obliterating civilizations. Earth's satellites detected a significant energy surge, signaling that the Domicans were powering up their ultimate weapon.

"Sir, we have a serious problem," Amayra informed General Bakshi. "The Domicans are preparing to use the Equalizer. We've recorded an energy build-up from their fleet."

"This is a grave situation," Bakshi responded, his face grim. "We have no way to counter their weapon directly. We must rely on Raj and his team. Until then, we need to stall them. Prepare all remaining ships and fighters, and call every squadron to the hangar."

As the human forces scrambled to ready themselves for what could be their final stand, General Bakshi delivered a stirring address.

"I know our resources are limited and our numbers are few," Bakshi said, his voice steady and resolute. "But our will and courage are our greatest assets. Courage is not the absence of fear but the understanding that something is more important than fear. Brave may not live forever, but the cautious don't live at all. We need to stall the Equalizer's activation until Raj arrives with the Lucifer. Report to your group leaders and prepare for battle."

The fighters charged up, fueled by Bakshi's inspiring words. "Prepare my ship," Bakshi ordered, his determination unshaken.

"But Sir, a commanding officer should not be in the field during a war," protested a subordinate.

"I understand that," Bakshi replied firmly. "But I refuse to stay idle. I will stand with my men, and if we fall, we fall together."

The human fleet ascended into the sky, forming a wave of fighters moving toward the Domican ships. The Domicans, caught off guard, deployed their own ships in response, but the sheer number of human fighters gave the defenders an advantage.

"The Domican shields are down due to the power being diverted to the Equalizer," one of Bakshi's officers noted. "But even if we reach their Mothership, we lack the means to destroy it."

"I know," Bakshi agreed. "We must hope that Raj arrives in time. His hologram is down, so he must be in hyperspace. Until then, we need to keep them distracted and slow down their weapon's charging."

The Domican High Commander, observing the human forces closing in, ordered his own ship to be prepared. "Prepare my ship. I will deal with these insects myself," he commanded, his tone brooking no argument.

The High Commander's ship was sleek and formidable, with a transponder-shaped cockpit and thin, efficient wings. It moved with precision; its weapons capable of dismantling human ships with ease.

"General, is that the Domican High Commander's ship?" a wingman asked.

"Yes, it is," Bakshi confirmed. "Finally, the big guy comes into play. Leave him to me. Stick to the plan and keep moving forward."

The High Commander's ship tore through the ranks of human fighters with deadly accuracy. "I'll handle him," Bakshi declared. "Keep following the plan."

As the Domican Mothership's guns came online, the Equalizer continued charging. Just then, a loud boom echoed through space as a new warship appeared from hyperspace. "That's Raj!" General Bakshi exclaimed. "He made it!"

The Lucifer, accompanied by the Phantom, emerged into the fray. The human fleet's morale surged as the advanced ship charged into the battle, its speed and firepower a game-changer. Raj launched ion torpedoes, causing significant damage to the Domican Mothership's defenses and disabling the Equalizer.

With the mothership offline and its equalizer system disabled, Phantom executed a tactial maneuver, circling back to launch nukes that struck the Mothership, causing an explosion so immense it resembled a supernova. The blast was visible from both Earth and Mars, marking a turning point in the battle.

This event ignited widespread celebrations across both Planets. Mars initiated a counteroffensive against Domicans , who were thrown into the disarray by the catastrophic events . Even the Moon base observed the spectacles via satellite, joining the celebrations.

Raj and the High Commander were locked in an intense dogfight. The High Commander was relentlessly tailing Raj, whose expert flying skills kept him barely ahead "Raj lead him towards me, I am sending my co-ordinates to you. Release flares when you are 15 meters away and execute a C-2" General Bakshi instructed over a private comm link. The C-2 was an aerial maneuver Raj had perfected earlier in his career unofficially taught but mastered through his own experience.

"A C-2, roger that General" Raj confirmed, rerouting all power to his rear deflectors to evade the High Commander's relentless fire. Following orders, he circled back to General Bakshi, deployed flares, and skilfully executed the C-2, disengaging his engines and deploying his jet's safety parachutes. This maneuver caused him to drift backwards in space at high speed. The High Commander, caught off-guard watched as saw Raj's jet grazed the front of his ship, damaging it. Just as the commander refocused, two incoming tropes struck his craft, sending him plummeting to his demise.

Raj, now free, manually deployed his parachutes and moved to complete his mission. He launched last of his Ion tropes at the Mothership. The hit was so precise it felt as though divine intervention had guided it. The resulting explosion dwarfed the previous one, incapacitating the Domican fleet. The fighters dropped out of the sky like flies, their shields disabled, allowing Earth's forces to easily overpower the retreating Domicans on both Earth and

Mars.

With the Mothership destroyed, the remaining Domican forces were left vulnerable. The Earth and Mars forces, now united, launched a relentless counterattack. Within two days, the Domicans were hunted down with the help of the Intergalactic Corps, and only a few managed to escape.

EPILOGUE: A NEW DAWN

Raj returned to the base to a hero's welcome. His brother Anuj and Amayra were waiting for him. Anuj ran to embrace Raj, tears of joy streaming down his face. Then, Raj noticed Amayra waiting for him, holding a bouquet of flowers and dressed in an elegant white gown. She hugged him so tightly he struggled to catch his breath.

"I'm happy to see you too," Raj gasped. "But you're squeezing me too tight!"

"I'm sorry," Amayra said, tears in her eyes.

"Is this bouquet for me?"

"This bouquet is for us." She replied

Raj looked puzzled. "I don't understand."

Amayra knelt down and proposed, "Will you marry me, Raj?"

Raj was momentarily stunned but then his shock turned to joy. "YES!" he shouted, jumping with excitement, his initial shock gave way to overwhelming joy as he jumped up and down like a child. Anuj then approached Raj, presenting him with a blue diamond crystal ring.

Raj then knelt, holding out a ring. "When I first saw you, it wasn't love at first sight. But over time, I noticed your hair, your eyes, your humor, your personality. Slowly but surely, I realized you are everything I needed. Amayra Mehra, will you marry me?"

The base erupted in applause. General Bakshi announced that the base would host the wedding, and all personnel's families were invited. The atmosphere was one of joy and celebration, a welcome reprieve from the devastation of war.

SIX MONTHS LATER

Earth and Mars were on the mend, gradually returning to a state of normalcy. Reconstruction efforts were underway, with memorials erected to honor those lost. Families began to heal, and the governments, in collaboration with Intergalactic War Foundation, provided compensation and support to affected families.

On Mars, the recovery was slower than on Earth due to the more extensive damage inflicted as a message of war. Prime Minister Mahendra Singh and other leaders, aided by public efforts, worked tirelessly to rebuild. Achal Mehta's company played a significant role in the recovery efforts.

Back on Earth, Raj and Amayra were happily married. Their wedding, as promised by General Bakshi, was a grand event hosted on the New Delhi base. Afterwards Raj and Amayra settled in their hometown of New Mumbai, living in a luxurious apartment gifted by the world government.

Raj had been promoted to Lieutenant General and oversaw the Mumbai base, while Amayra, now Chief Supervising Analyst in the Air Force, continued her critical work.

Earth's defense, which was proven inadequate during the war, were significantly upgraded, as Earth and Mars prepared for future challenges, their heroes remained vigilant. The legacy of the war lived on, a testament to the courage and resilience of those who fought to save their worlds. Though peace prevailed for the moment, Earth and its heroes stood ready for ant challenges that might arise in the future.

www.ingramcontent.com/pod-product-compliance
Lightning Source LLC
LaVergne TN
LVHW041238150826
845673LV00008B/2422

* 9 7 9 8 8 9 5 8 8 8 6 3 6 *